I Love a Book

Books Are Fun envisions a world where every child, regardless of background, has access to a vibrant home library, fostering a lifelong journey of learning, imagination, and personal growth. Through dynamic partnerships with schools, we aim to turn every home into a nurturing space filled with the wonders of literature, ensuring that the joy and benefits of reading touch every family, building brighter futures, and inspiring life long readers one book at a time.

I Love a Book

Joe Rhatigan

Illustrated by Olga & Aleksey Ivanov

creative
publishing services

There are books to treasure
or return when you're done,

books that are serious,
and books that are fun.

On the cover of one book I see
what looks like an exciting mystery.
There is a ship, but where's the crew?
There's only one thing for me to do. . .

I turn the pages and read them fast.
Will this story last and last?
Did pirates really sail the sea
and say, "Aargh" and "Ahoy matey"?

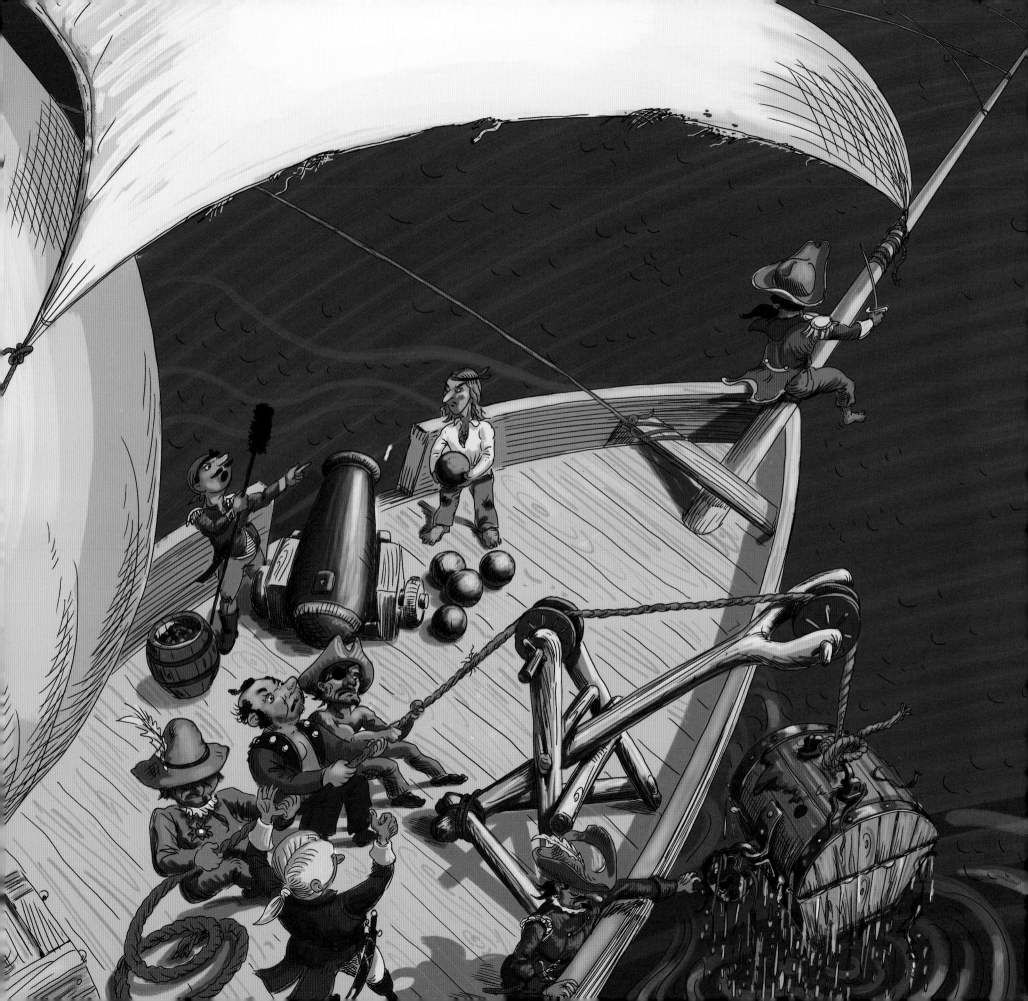

And what's it like to fly so high
that you suddenly run out of sky?
Do aliens read books like me?
Who knows? Find a book fast and see!

Look here! It's an animal doctor
who makes house calls in a helicopter.
And how did a cow get up that tree?
Books have the answers, I guarantee!

Take a peek and have a look.
Wonders abound when you open a book.
Robots with top hats up in the clouds,
frogs of rare talent singing to crowds,

Monsters learning to count
on their powerful paws,
and sharks chewing gum
with their dangerous jaws.

This book lists all the dogs in the land. In the next one, ancient Egyptians build pyramids in sand.

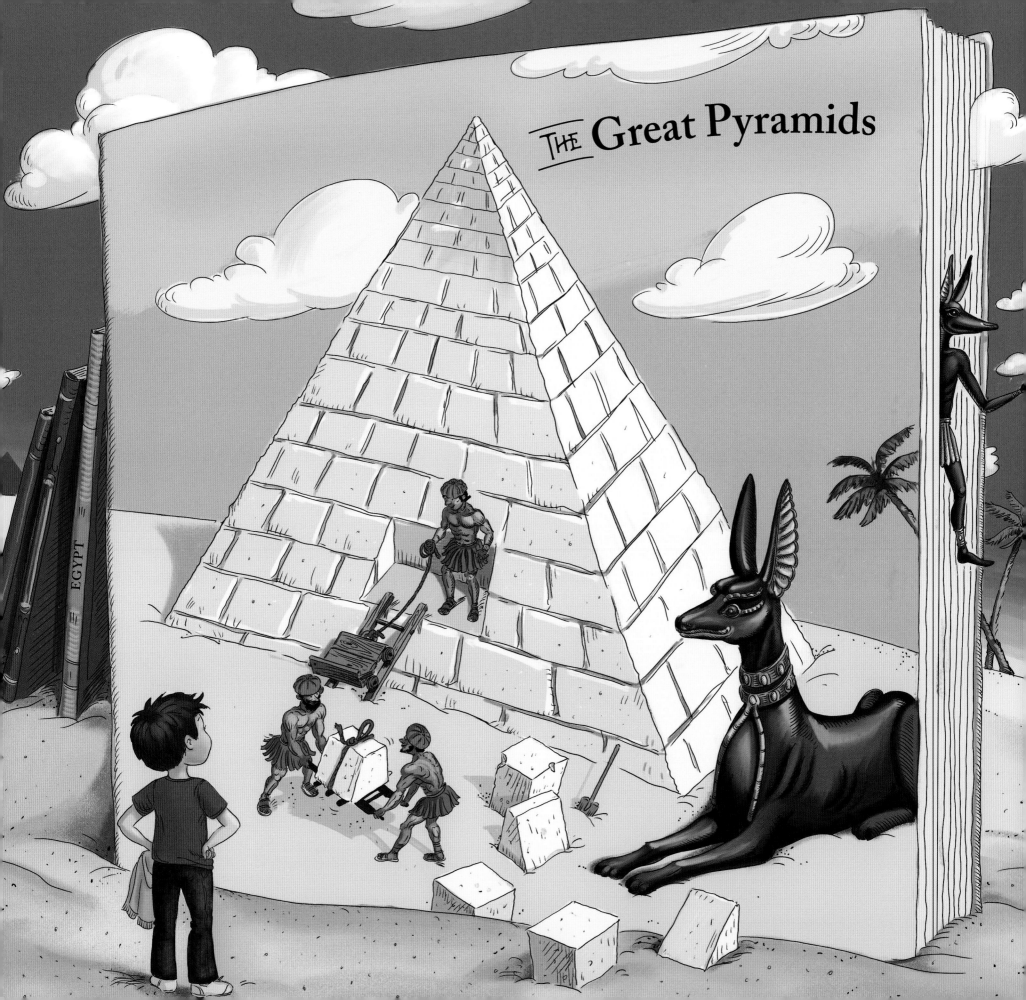

The Great Pyramids

Each book is like a magical net
that captures stories so we never forget.
Up on the shelves the books stand by,
waiting for us so their ideas can fly.

And it's silly that my parents think
they can use all this magical paper and ink
to quiet me down at the end of the day.
"There's too much to read!" I eagerly say.

Then just before bedtime, when day turns to night,
I plead, "Just one more book before you turn off the light!"

Tonight I am lucky ... we read three or four.
(And if I hadn't fallen asleep, we would have read more.)

Published by Creative Publishing Services, Morganville, NJ 07751, USA

www.creativepubservices.com

ISBN 979-8-9876196-9-8

Printed in China, August 2024

10 9 8 7 6 5 4 3 2 1

For information about custom editions, special sales, and premium and corporate purchases,
please contact Creative Publishing Services at info@creativepublishingservices.com.

This edition printed exclusively for Books Are Fun, 2024.
First edition published in 2017 by MoonDance Press, an imprint of The Quarto Group.

Cover design and layout by Melissa Gerber